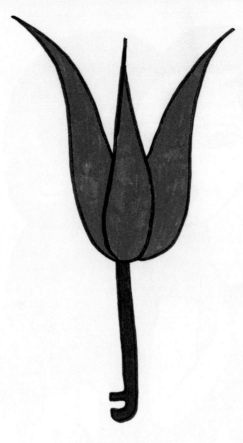

Magical Key

Two handsome Khmer Princes,

Sokhen and Sokhit, worshipped

the Jade Princess Andevi

Bassarangchmur,

Sokhen

who in turn, gave them a magical key.

Taking the key and burning it upon an altar,

a haloed portal appeared.

Prostrating themselves before Andevi,

she transformed them into ravens

Sokhit

And the prince-birds flew through the portal

Foot Emerging From Royal-Sky Fruit

to a bizarre and mysterious world where

countless feet with unusual soles

inhabited the eerie landscape.

Worshipping the Jade Princess once more,

both men changed back to their normal selves.

Vaginal Sole Of Foot

Hoping to appease Andevi, Sokhen and

Sokhit gathered several feet and

went into them.

NeoKhmer Red

So the Jade Princess made these

feet into gorgeous women.

NeoKhmer Blue

She named the inhabitants NeoKhmer

and crowned the two Princes as their Kings.

Order this book online at www.trafford.com
or email orders@trafford.com

Most Trafford titles are also available at major online book retailers.

 www.trafford.com

North America & international
toll-free: 844 688 6899 (USA & Canada)
fax: 812 355 4082

Our mission is to efficiently provide the world's finest, most comprehensive book publishing service, enabling every author to experience success. To find out how to publish your book, your way, and have it available worldwide, visit us online at www.trafford.com

Because of the dynamic nature of the Internet, any web addresses or links contained in this book may have changed since publication and may no longer be valid. The views expressed in this work are solely those of the author and do not necessarily reflect the views of the publisher, and the publisher hereby disclaims any responsibility for them.

ISBN: 978-1-4120-9150-3 (sc)

Print information available on the last page.

Trafford rev. 03/04/2021

Printed in the United States
by Baker & Taylor Publisher Services